Wink

THE NINJA WHO WANTED TO NAP

BY J. C. PHILLIPPS

VIKING

An Imprint of Penguin Group (USA) Inc.

Wink was a ninja who wanted to be noticed.

And he was noticed every day as the star of the Lucky Dragon Circus.

He performed as the Nimble Ninja in towns all over Japan.

But now it was time to take a break. Wink and Grandmother returned to their own village and waved good-bye to the other circus performers.

Wink was excited to see his old teacher, Master Zutsu, and his friends at the Summer Moon School for Young Ninjas.

Reporters arrived to interview Wink for *Popular Ninja* magazine. Wink flipped, kicked, and tumbled down the Hall of Noble Battles.

"Isn't this great?" he asked Master Zutsu. "I'm the most famous ninja in the world!"

"A golden cage is still a cage," Master Zutsu muttered.

Wink was about to do a tornado flip when a yawn escaped his mouth—*mwaaa*.

Grandmother swooped in. "Sometimes it is good to be noticed," she said. "And sometimes it is good to nap."

Outside Grandmother's house, three fans were waiting for him. "I'm Ikuko," said a girl dressed in her school uniform. "These are my friends, Midori and Takai."

Wink signed autographs
and posed for pictures until
another yawn slipped out.

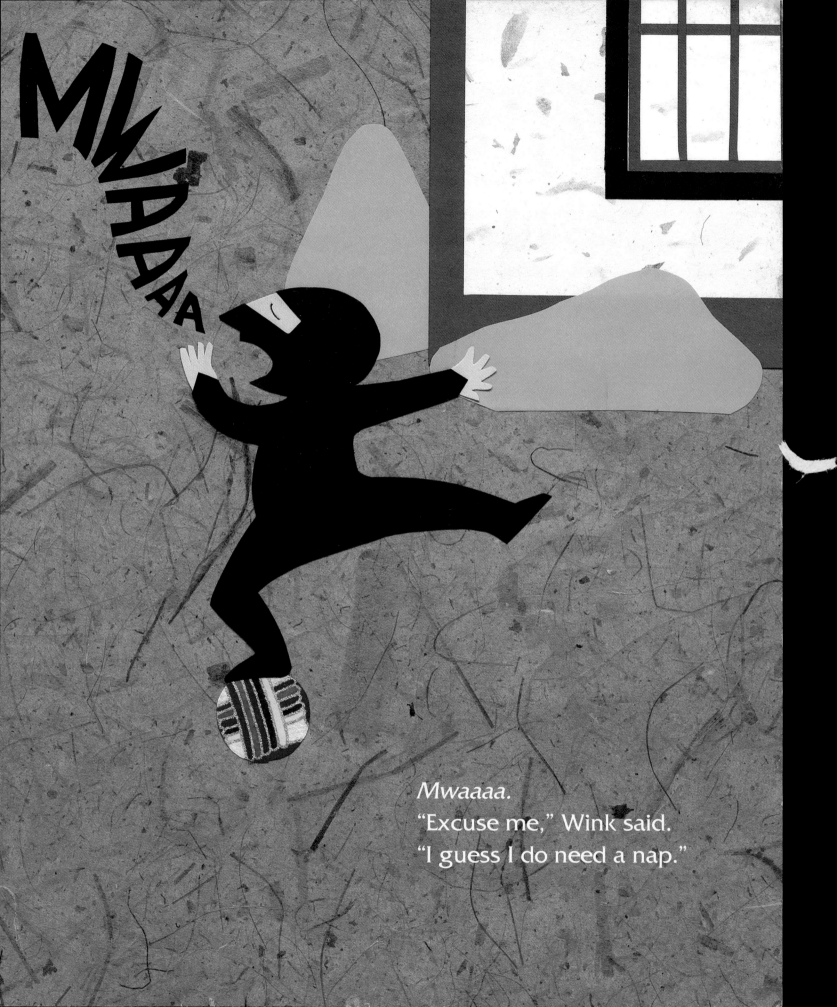

Mwaaaa.
"Excuse me," Wink said.
"I guess I do need a nap."

Inside, Grandmother rolled out his futon. "Rest well, Wink-chan," she said. "Stroll along the path of dreams."

Wink closed his eyes. Then he heard whispering. Three faces peeked in the window.

"Uh, hello," Wink said. He wanted the fans to leave, but he didn't want to be rude. "I'm trying to sleep. Could you come back later?"

Midori giggled.

"That was a short journey,"
Grandmother said.

Wink rubbed his eyes.
"I couldn't fall asleep."

He spied a pair of pigtails in
the window and got an idea.

"Grandmother," Wink
said in a loud voice. "A
walk through the Damasu
Gardens will calm me."

The pigtails disappeared.

Wink smiled and winked.

Wink meandered through the garden gates.

He weaved through cherry blossom trees.

Then he dashed ahead and hid beneath a bridge.
"I'm a super ninja," Wink said as he hurried home.

Halfway there, Wink stopped to yawn. *Mwaaa.*
He heard a giggle.

"*Shimatta!*" Wink said, and stomped his foot. *Shoot!*

Wink ran ahead
and tried to hide
at the bike shop . . .

the toy store . . .

and the market.

But the fans found him.

Wink crawled, jumped, and spun through town, trying to escape from the three fans.

But Wink couldn't help being noticed, and more and more followers joined along the way. Until . . .

. . . Wink found himself back
at the Summer Moon School
for Young Ninjas.

MASTER ZUTSU!

"Master Zutsu!" Wink called.

He found his old teacher practicing the art of calligraphy.

Wink explained his problem.

"I want to go home and nap, but my fans won't leave me alone." Wink yawned. "I guess when I'm sleepy, I'm no good at stealth."

Master Zutsu rolled his eyes.

"Come," Master Zutsu said, and led Wink to the training yard.

"One zebra alone is easily seen. A herd creates confusion."

Why can't Master Zutsu say anything normal?
Wink thought. Then he got an idea.

"Hey! If my ninja friends run around like fake
Winks," he said, "the fans will get mixed up and
chase them instead of me. Then I can go home
and nap!"

Three ninjas burst out of the front gate and ran through the crowd.

"Which one is Wink?" Takai asked.

"I don't know," said Ikuko. "We'd better split up."

Ikuko's group followed a ninja to the fabric shop.

Takai's group chased a ninja through the zoo.

Midori's group cornered a ninja wearing glasses.
"You're not Wink," she said.

By the time the fans finally made it to Wink's house, he had just awakened from a two-hour snooze.

"You look beat," Wink said.
"I think you all need a nap."

For Cameron, who rarely naps

VIKING
Published by Penguin Group
Penguin Young Readers Group, 345 Hudson Street, New York, New York 10014, U.S.A.
Penguin Group (Canada), 90 Eglinton Avenue East, Suite 700, Toronto, Ontario, Canada M4P 2Y3
(a division of Pearson Penguin Canada Inc.)
Penguin Books Ltd, 80 Strand, London WC2R 0RL, England
Penguin Ireland, 25 St Stephen's Green, Dublin 2, Ireland (a division of Penguin Books Ltd)
Penguin Group (Australia), 250 Camberwell Road, Camberwell, Victoria 3124, Australia
(a division of Pearson Australia Group Pty Ltd)
Penguin Books India Pvt Ltd, 11 Community Centre, Panchsheel Park, New Delhi – 110 017, India
Penguin Group (NZ), 67 Apollo Drive, Rosedale, North Shore 0632, New Zealand
(a division of Pearson New Zealand Ltd)
Penguin Books (South Africa) (Pty) Ltd, 24 Sturdee Avenue, Rosebank, Johannesburg 2196, South Africa

First published in 2011 by Viking, a division of Penguin Young Readers Group

1 3 5 7 9 10 8 6 4 2

Copyright © J. C. Phillipps, 2011
All rights reserved

LIBRARY OF CONGRESS CATALOGING-IN-PUBLICATION DATA IS AVAILABLE
ISBN 978-0-670-01192-6

Manufactured in China
Set in Alliance
Book design by Sam Kim